A PREDICTABLE WORD BOOK

THE TUB THAT BECAME A BOAT

Story by Janie Spaht Gill, Ph.D.
Illustrations by Bob Reese

 ARO PUBLISHING

Bobby filled the tub
to sail his sail boat.

The tub became a boat and began to float.

It floated off the floor.

It floated out the door.

It floated down the stairs.

13

14

It floated between some chairs.

It floated around the block.

17

It floated toward the dock.

19

Bobby screamed, "Whee!"

21

As he floated out to sea!

23